Yasmeen Ismail

Kiki and Bobo's Sunny Day

D1336785

Kiki and Bobo were having breakfast.
"It's so sunny this morning, Bobo," said Kiki.
"Do you know where I would like to go?"
"Where would you like to go, Kiki?" asked Bobo.
"To the seaside!" said Kiki.

Kiki packed her swimsuit and
put on her rubber ring.
"Where is your swimsuit, Bobo?" asked Kiki.

"I've lost it and I'm not sure I
will swim today," said Bobo.
"Maybe it's under your hat," said Kiki.

Bobo was very quiet on the bus to the beach. "I am so excited to swim in the sea," said Kiki. Bobo was not excited to swim in the sea. He wanted to go home.

"Let's have an ice cream," said Kiki.
"One for me, and one for you, Bobo."
Bobo did not feel like eating his ice cream
and he dropped it in the sand.

"Don't worry, Bobo," said Kiki.
"You can have some of mine."

"Shall we swim now, Bobo?" asked Kiki.
"No, Kiki," said Bobo, "we must put our
    sun cream on first."
"Good idea Bobo,"
    said Kiki.

"Now shall we go swimming?" asked Kiki.
"No, Kiki, I would like to look for some shells first," said Bobo.

So they collected seashells all along the shore.

"Let's go swimming now!" said Kiki.
"No, Kiki," said Bobo, "I think we should make a big sandcastle now."
"OK, Bobo," said Kiki, "but I want to go swimming soon."

"Now it's time for swimming!" shouted Kiki.
"What's wrong, Bobo?"

"I'm scared of swimming in the sea," said Bobo, and he started to cry. Poor Bobo.

"Don't worry, Bobo," said Kiki. "You can use my rubber ring, and I'll stay with you the whole time. Would you like that?"

"Yes, Kiki," said Bobo, "I would like that very much." Kiki held Bobo's hand all the way into the sea. "I'm swimming, Kiki!" shouted Bobo.

That evening Kiki and Bobo
had a bath and then had tea.
"Thank you for helping me to swim, Kiki,"
said Bobo. "I'm not scared any more."